"It's July!" said Mark.

"Gran's birthday is July 6!"

"I know what I'll do!" he said.

"I won't wrap a gift. I'll write a letter!"

"First, I'll write a rough draft,"
said Mark.

"Then I'll see if it's good enough."

Mark began to write and write.

"Good!" said Mark. "Now I'll write my name. Then I'll mail this before Gran's birthday."

On July 6 Gran got the letter.
"I know who this is from!" she said.